TRACTOR MAC

CERTIFICATE OF REGISTRATION

· · ·

This book belongs to

_____

TRACTOR MAC
HARVEST TIME

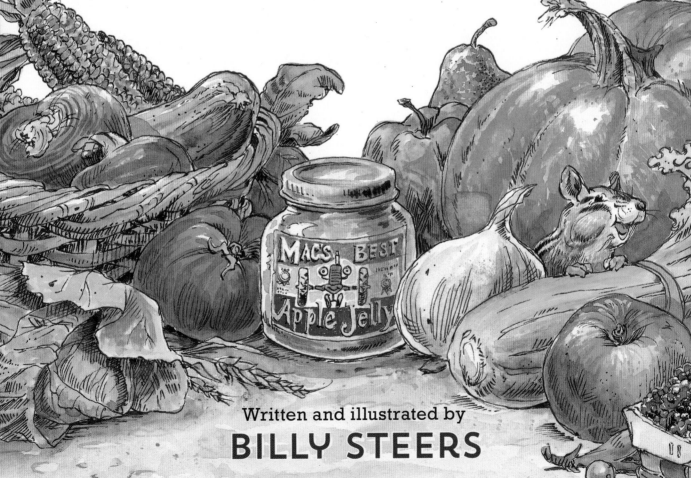

MAC'S BEST
Apple Jelly

Written and illustrated by
BILLY STEERS

FARRAR STRAUS GIROUX • **NEW YORK**

T

RACTOR MAC NOTICED IT FIRST.
The nights were getting cooler, the corn was ready
to harvest, and the huge orange pumpkin-patch signs
were set up across the road from Stony Meadow Farm.

It was time for the neighboring farm's Pumpkin Picking Festival!
Every fall, children from all over come to ride the hay wagon that
Small Fred the tractor pulls up and down the hills to his pumpkin
patch. People pick their pumpkins, and Small Fred takes them
back to the farm stand for refreshments and games.

"It must be fun to watch the children try to guess the big pumpkin's weight or find their way through the hay maze," said Mac. "I wish we had a pumpkin-picking festival at Stony Meadow Farm. The hayrides! All the happy children! All the big pumpkins!"

"You will have to bring in the apples to the cider mill," Sibley the horse reminded him. "It's that time of year, too, you know."

Mac shuddered. "The apple orchard! Ugh!" Mac remembered last fall in the apple orchard. His exhaust stack caught on limbs. His big tires tangled in the branches. Apples fell off the trees when he passed and made him sticky. "Yes, it's that time of year, too," said Mac with a sigh.

Small Fred had seen the "Apple Time" sign go up across the road at Stony Meadow Farm. "Oh, no—it must also be time for the Pumpkin Picking Festival," Small Fred said to Pepper the cat. "I can barely pull this hay wagon. The pumpkins are too heavy, and the children are too noisy.

"It's not peaceful and quiet like that beautiful apple orchard," Small Fred added.

"It's that time of year, Fred," Pepper meowed.

Tractor Mac wove through the apple trees the following day. "I'm just too big for this small orchard!" he groaned to Sibley the horse. Branches poked his grille and nearly toppled his exhaust stack.

"Apples are a useful crop," said Sibley. "You can make applesauce, apple pies, apple cider, apple cider vinegar . . ."

"Okay, okay," said Mac. "It's just that—" *WUMP!* Mac's big tire hit an apple tree. Tractor Mac and Farmer Bill were showered with apples.

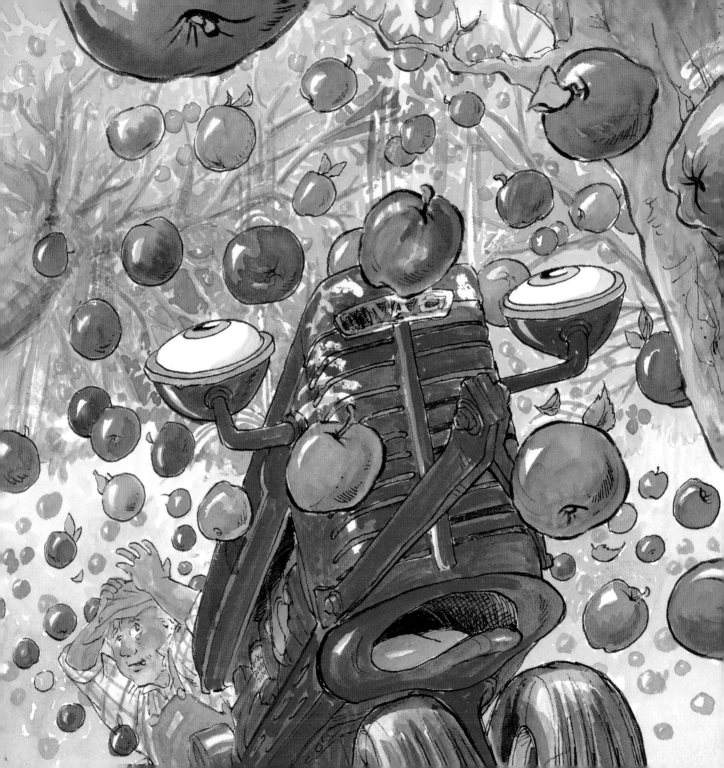

Farmer Bill put Tractor Mac in reverse to back up. *WUMP!* Another apple tree dumped its apples. "Hold on, Mac," said Farmer Bill with a laugh, "or we'll have nothing but applesauce left!"

"You look smashing!" buzzed the bees.

Back at the cider mill, Farmer
Bill washed off the apple pulp from
Tractor Mac while the big cider
press worked away.

"You're not the only one having a hard time today, Mac," said Sam the ram. "Look at Small Fred over there." Mac could see customers unloading their pumpkins from Fred's wagon. Small Fred couldn't pull the heavy load back up the hill to the farm stand.

"Hmmm," Farmer Bill said. "You know, a pumpkin patch has much more room to move around in, Mac. I think there may be a better job for a big tractor like you."

Mac wheeled down the hill, across the road, and over to where Small Fred sat with his half-empty wagon.

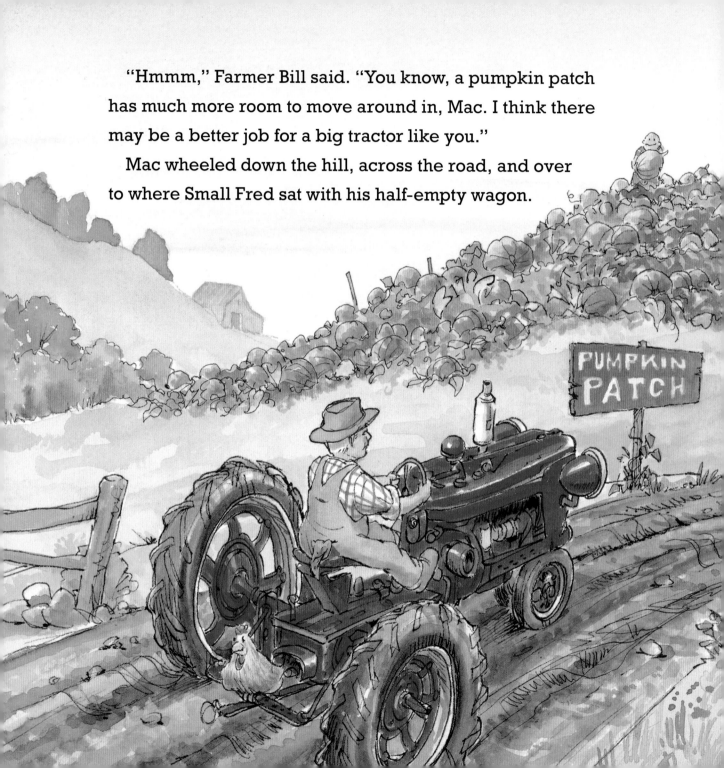

Soon Mac was pulling the pumpkin wagon loaded with
happy, singing passengers up the hill to the farm stand.
"Hooray!" shouted the children.

Small Fred went across the road to the apple orchard at Stony Meadow Farm. "You fit perfectly under the apple trees," hummed the bees.

Small Fred was very happy. The air smelled of apples, and the orchard was peaceful and quiet.

At the end of the day, everyone met back at the Pumpkin Picking Festival. Farmer Bill and Small Fred brought apple cider to share. Small Fred's owner gave Farmer Bill and Tractor Mac the biggest, grandest pumpkin from the pumpkin patch.

"I'm glad we could help each other out," Small Fred said.

"We got to share the work and share the fun!" said Tractor Mac.

To the Bronson family of Maple Bank Farm.

May all your harvests be bountiful!

Farrar Straus Giroux Books for Young Readers
175 Fifth Avenue, New York 10010

Copyright © 2007 by Billy Steers
All rights reserved
Color separations by Bright Arts (H.K.) Ltd.
Printed in China by Toppan Leefung Printing Ltd.,
Dongguan City, Guangdong Province
Designed by Kristie Radwilowicz
Previous edition published by Tractor Mac, LLC
First Farrar Straus Giroux edition, 2015
1 3 5 7 9 10 8 6 4 2

mackids.com

Library of Congress Cataloging-in-Publication Data
Steers, Billy, author, illustrator.
Tractor Mac, harvest time / Billy Steers. —First Farrar Straus Giroux edition.
pages cm
Originally published in Roxbury, Connecticut, by Tractor Mac in 2007.
Summary: Tractor Mac and friends celebrate autumn festivals.
ISBN 978-0-374-30111-8 (paper over board)
[1. Tractors—Fiction.   2. Autumn—Fiction.   3. Harvest festivals—Fiction.]   I. Title.   II.
Title: Harvest time.

PZ7.S81536Tqt 2015
[E]—dc23

2014040393

Farrar Straus Giroux Books for Young Readers may be purchased for business or promotional
use. For information on bulk purchases please contact Macmillan Corporate and Premium
Sales Department at (800) 221-7945 x5442 or by email at specialmarkets@macmillan.com.

ABOUT THE AUTHOR

Billy Steers is an author, illustrator, and commercial pilot. In addition to the Tractor Mac series, he has worked on forty other children's books. Mr. Steers had horses and sheep on the farm where he grew up in Connecticut. Married with three sons, he still lives in Connecticut. Learn more about the Tractor Mac books at www.tractormac.com.

Tractor Mac™